A Hot Thirsty Day

Marjorie Weinman Sharmat

pictures by Rosemary Wells

The Macmillan Company, New York

COLLIER-MACMILLAN LTD., LONDON

Printed in the United States of America

The Macmillan Company
866 Third Avenue, New York, New York 10022

Collier-Macmillan Canada Ltd., Toronto, Ontario

Library of Congress Catalog Card Number: 70-123130

10 9 8 7 6 5 4 3 2 1

For Uncle Ned

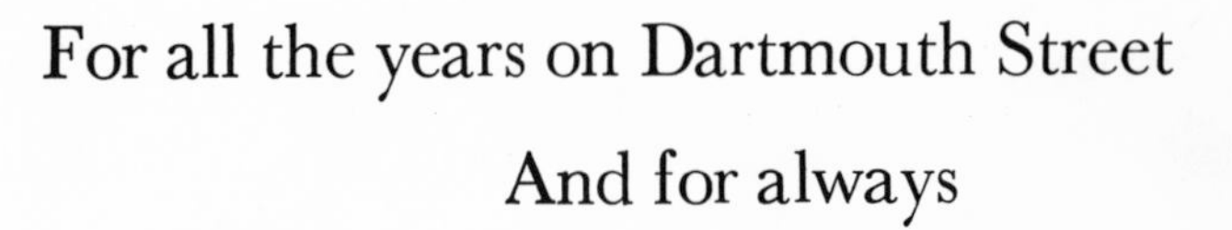

For all the years on Dartmouth Street

And for always

Tommy and Jon and Mitchell were sitting under a tree.

"Who has a dime?" asked Tommy.

Mitchell looked in Tommy's right pocket.

He looked in Tommy's left pocket.

He looked under Tommy's cap.

"You don't have a dime," he said.

"I know I don't," said Tommy. "That's why I asked for one."

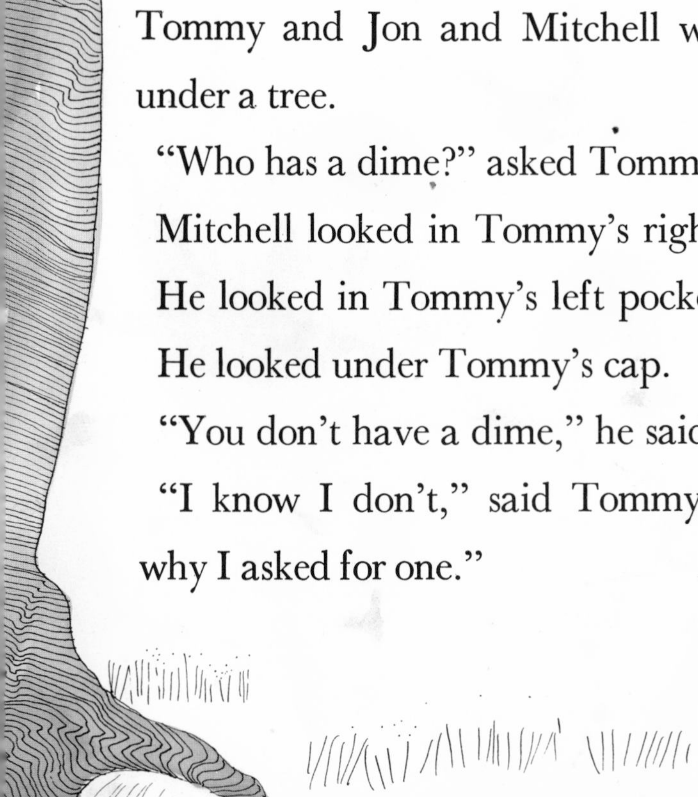

"If I had a dime, I would have spent it," said Jon.

"I have three dimes," said Mitchell.

"You do?" said Tommy.

"Yes," said Mitchell. "They're in my piggy bank."

"Can you get them?" asked Jon.

"Sure," said Mitchell. "Nobody is home. The key is outside in the geranium pot. I'll go home, get the key and open the door. I'll get a ladder from the cellar and take it to my room. I'll climb the ladder to the top shelf of my closet and take my piggy bank down. I'll break the piggy bank with a hammer and take out the three dimes. Then I'll bring them here."

"Never mind," said Jon. "There must be an easier way to get money."

"I know," said Tommy. "Let's start a business."

"Good idea," said Mitchell. "How about the spy business?"

"You need a trench coat for that," said Jon. "Do you have a trench coat?"

"My father has one," said Mitchell. "But he isn't a spy. He's a milkman."

"Think of another business," said Tommy.

"I know," said Jon. "The chocolate ice cream business."

"Chocolate ice cream isn't a business," said Tommy. "You have to sell all the flavors."

"I only like chocolate," said Jon.

"Think some more," said Tommy.

"I can't think of anything as good as the chocolate ice cream business," said Jon.

"I know," said Mitchell. "The lemonade business."

"No," said Tommy.

"No," said Jon. "There are three lemonade stands on this block."

"Keep thinking," said Tommy.

They thought about the lawn-mowing business.

"Too hard," said Tommy.

They thought about the snow-shoveling business.

"No snow," said Jon.

"The lemonade business is a good business," said Mitchell.

"No," said Tommy.

"No," said Jon.

They thought about selling worms.

They thought about selling old toys.

And Mitchell thought about selling his geraniums.

Nothing seemed right.

"The lemonade business is a good business," said Mitchell.

Tommy looked at Jon. Jon looked at Tommy. Then they all walked to Tommy's house. They took some things from the refrigerator. They took some things from a shelf. They took some things from the cellar, the laundry room and a wastebasket.

They went back outside. They pasted, painted, hammered and pasted some more.

LEMON-
ADE

LEMON
ADE

And they started the fourth lemonade stand on the block.

"I'm in charge of the lemons, sugar, water and ice," said Jon.

"And I'm in charge of the money," said Tommy.

"The lemonade looks good," said Mitchell. "I think I'll be in charge of tasting it."

"No," said Tommy. "You're in charge of stirring. You stir the lemon juice, sugar, water and ice."

"All right," said Mitchell. "But I'm a better taster than stirrer."

"Here come three ladies," said Tommy. "Now stand straight and smile."

"Hello," said one of the ladies. "It's a nice day."

"Yes," said Mitchell. "It's a nice, thirsty, hot, thirsty day." And he stirred hard. The ice cubes clinked.

"A very nice day," said the other ladies. And they walked on.

"They didn't buy any lemonade," said Tommy.

Two men came along. Tommy and Jon stood straight and smiled. Mitchell stirred hard. The ice cubes clanked.

The men walked right by.

Tommy stopped smiling. "Business is terrible," he said.

"We can still sell my geraniums," said Mitchell.

"Maybe our lemonade costs too much," said Jon.

"Say, maybe you're right," said Tommy. "Let's find out how much it costs at the other stands on the block."

"Who'll go and find out?" asked Jon. He looked at Mitchell.

"I don't know," said Tommy. And he looked at Mitchell, too.

"I'll go," said Mitchell. "My arm is tired from stirring."

He ran down the street. Soon he came running back around the other end of the block.

"I was right," he said. "It's a nice, thirsty, hot, thirsty day. I need some lemonade."

"What did you find out?" asked Tommy.

"I found out that I don't need a trench coat to be a spy," said Mitchell. "They told me I was a spy."

"Did you find out what their lemonade costs?" asked Jon.

"Seven cents a glass," said Mitchell.

"Very good," said Tommy. "Our lemonade will cost less. Our lemonade will cost six cents a glass."

Some girls walked down the street. Mitchell stirred hard. But all the ice had melted.

"Look," said one of the girls. "Only six cents a glass for lemonade. It costs seven cents at the other stands."

The girls bought four glasses.

LEMON
ADE
8¢
6¢

"Four glasses at six cents a glass," said Tommy. "We made twenty-four cents."

A woman with a cat came along. "One glass of lemonade, please," she said. She took a saucer from her pocketbook. She poured the lemonade into the saucer. "My cat loves lemonade," she said.

The cat lapped up all the lemonade in the saucer.

"Would you like some, too?" asked Tommy.

"No," she said. "I only drink milk."

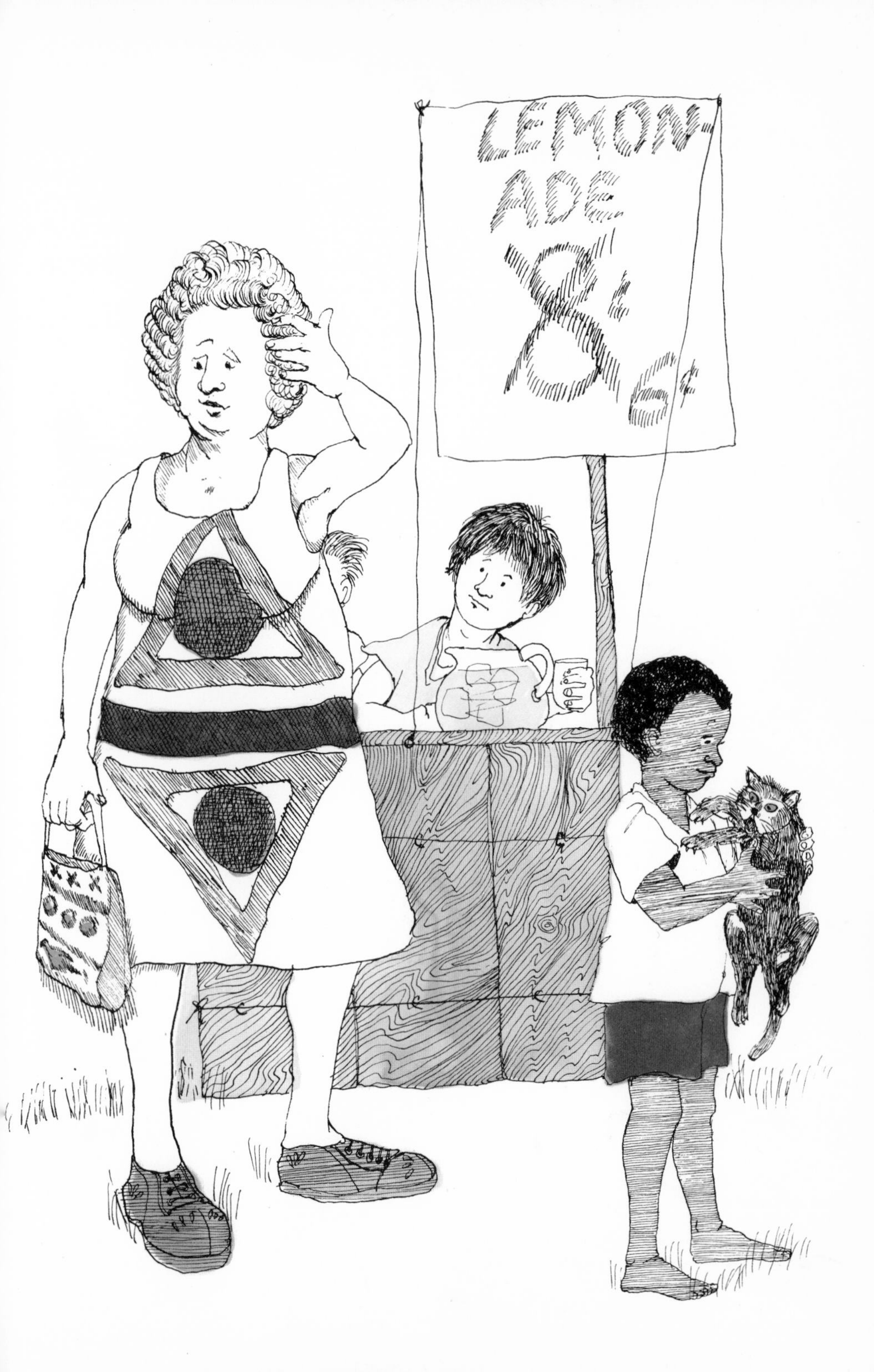
LEMON-
ADE
8¢
6¢

She picked up the empty saucer. She put it back in her pocketbook, picked up her cat and walked away.

"Another six cents," said Tommy. "Now we have twenty-four cents and six cents. That makes thirty cents."

"Here come three boys," said Jon.

Mitchell looked at the boys. Then he ducked behind the lemonade sign.

The boys walked up to the stand. "I'm Charlie," said one of them. "Some girls told us that you sell lemonade for six cents a glass."

"That's right," said Tommy. "Would you like some?"

Orioles

"We *have* some," said Charlie. "We own the other lemonade stands on the block."

"You do?" said Tommy.

"Do you?" said Jon.

Mitchell didn't say anything. He bent his head lower behind the sign.

"We sell lemonade for seven cents a glass," said Charlie. "You will spoil our business."

"We will?" said Tommy.

"Will we?" said Jon.

Mitchell knocked over the sign.

"It's the spy!" said Charlie.

"Hello," said Mitchell. "Would you like to buy a geranium?"

"No," said Charlie. "We'd like to buy your lemonade business."

"You would?" said Tommy.

"You know we put a lot of lemon and sugar into this business," said Mitchell. He looked at his arm. "And a lot of stirring, too. The price is seventy-five cents."

"We'll pay you forty-five cents," said Charlie.

"We'll take it," said Mitchell.

Mitchell, Tommy and Jon counted their money. "We've got a lot more than a dime," said Jon. "What did you want a dime for, Tommy?"

"I forget," said Tommy.

"Think," said Jon.

"A geranium costs about a dime," said Mitchell.

"No, it wasn't that," said Tommy.

"A chocolate ice cream?" said Jon.

"No, not that," said Tommy.

"I'm still thirsty," said Mitchell. "I think I'll buy some lemonade."

"That sounds good," said Tommy. "That sounds better than what I forgot. Let's all buy some."

And they did. Because it was a nice, thirsty, hot, thirsty day.